A Mouse in the House

by Vivian French

illustrated by Tim Archbold

READZONE

A Mouse in
the House

ReadZone Books Limited

50 Godfrey Avenue
Twickenham
TW2 7PF
UK

First published in this edition 2014

British Library Cataloguing in Publication Data (CIP) is available
for this title.

Printed in Malta by Melita Press

ISBN 978 1 78322 416 6

Visit our website: www.readzonebooks.com

"Somebody help me,
help me, please…

There's a mouse in
my house…

...and it's eating
my cheese!"

8

"Never mind, Gran — I've a cure for that. What you need is a black and white CAT!"

"Oh no! Oh no!

Where DID that cat go?

All that I've got today
in my house is a...

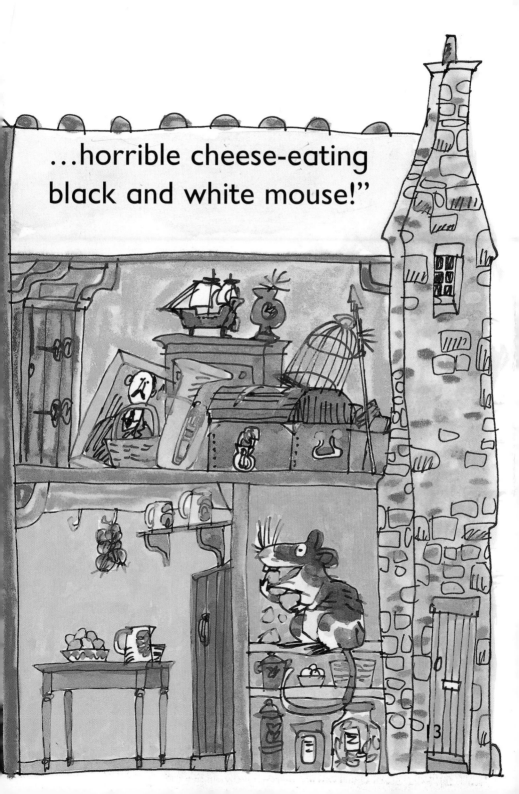

"Don't worry, Gran, I know what to do. A big spotty DOG is the thing for you!"

Where DID that dog go?

All that I've got today
in my house...

"Don't worry Gran,
I know what to do…

...a dear little FLEA
is the thing for you."

"Three cheers! That mouse has scurried away.

"Somebody help me!
Help me, please —

I'm itching and scratching...

Did you enjoy this book?

Look out for more *Redstarts* titles – first rhyming stories